LAURENCE ANHOLT has been described as "one of the most
versatile writers for children today" and was included in
The Independent On Sunday "Top 10 Children's Authors in Britain."
From his home in Lyme Regis, he has produced more than 90 children's
titles, which are published in dozens of languages around the world,
many of them in collaboration with his wife, Catherine.
His books range from the "Anholt Artists" series to the irrepressible
Chimp and Zee. Laurence has won numerous awards, including
the Nestlé Smarties Gold Award on two occasions.

Laurence and Catherine Anholt are the owners
of *Chimp and Zee, Bookshop by the Sea* in Lyme Regis.
Stocked entirely with their own signed books, prints, and cards,
and crammed with automated displays and book-related exhibits,
it is one of the most magical children's bookshops
you could ever hope to visit.

For my father, Gerry Anholt,
with love.

Text and illustrations copyright
© Laurence Anholt 1996

Degas and the Little Dancer was conceived,
edited, and produced by Frances Lincoln Ltd.,
4 Torriano Mews, Torriano Avenue, London NW5 2RZ

First edition for the United States,
Canada, and the Philippines published 1996
by Barron's Educational Series, Inc.

First published in Great Britain in 1996 by
Frances Lincoln Limited.

All inquiries should be addressed to:
Barron's Educational Series, Inc.
250 Wireless Boulevard
Hauppauge, New York 11788

The Library of Congress has catalogued the hardcover
editions as follows:
Library of Congress Catalog Card No. 95-42314

ISBN-13: 978-0-7641-3852-2

Library of Congress Cataloging-in-Publication Data
Anholt, Laurence.
Degas and the little dancer: a story about Edgar Degas/
by Laurence Anholt.
p.   cm.
Summary: Because Marie helps her poor parents
by modeling for an ill-tempered artist, she becomes
a famous ballerina but not in the way she had dreamed.
ISBN 0-8120-6583-2
[1. Ballet dancing—Fiction. 2. Degas, Edgar,
1834-1917—Fiction.] I. Title.
PZ7.A58635De 1996
[Fic]–dc20   95-42314
                 CIP
                 AC
Manufactured by South China Printing in Dongguan, Guangdong,
China in February 2014
19 18 17 16 15 14 13 12 11 10 9 8 7

Sculpture (Bronze and muslin):
THE LITTLE DANCER OF FOURTEEN YEARS 1880-81
(Musée d'Orsay, Paris © photos RMN)
Pictures of dancers (left to right):
GROUP OF DANCERS 1890's (National Gallery of
Scotland, Edinburgh: photo Bridgeman Art Library,
London); **DANCERS** (Heydt Museum, Wuppertal:
photo Bridgeman Art Library, London);
DANCER FASTENING HER PUMP c1880-85 (Private
Collection: photo Bridgeman Art Library, London);
DANCER AT REST c1880 (Private Collection: photo
Christie's, London/Bridgeman Art Library, London);
BLUE DANCERS c1897 (Pushkin Museum, Moscow:
photo Bridgeman Art Library, London);
PORTRAIT OF DEGAS c1890 (photo Bibliothèque
Nationale, Paris)

Degas

and the Little Dancer

A story
about **Edgar Degas**

by LAURENCE
ANHOLT

BARRON'S

In the middle of a big room, in a famous art museum,
is a beautiful sculpture of a little dancer. She stands with
one foot forward, her hands clasped behind her back.
She looks tired and a bit sad.

The sculpture was made more than a hundred years ago
by an artist called Edgar Degas.

The guard who looks after the room in the museum
has a story to tell about the little ballerina. When it
is raining outside and people have nowhere else to go,
someone is sure to ask who she was.

"Her name is Marie," says the guard. "I look
at her standing there everyday, and I think I know
her pretty well..."

. . . Marie and her parents were very poor, but Marie dreamed of only one thing—she wanted to be a dancer. Not just any dancer: she wanted to dance at the Paris Opera House. She wanted to be the most famous ballerina in the world.

Marie's father was a tailor and her mother took in
laundry. They worked hard and saved their money, until
the day Marie was ready to take the entrance exam for
the big ballet school.

Her father made her a special tutu, and her mother
wished her luck, and tied a long peach-colored ribbon
in her hair.

At the exam, Marie danced as she had never danced before, and the old ballet teacher seemed to like her.

"If we give you a place," he said, "you will have to practice very hard."

"I know," said Marie, "I want to be the most famous dancer in the world."

Everyone laughed. "We'll see about that!" said the old teacher.

It was the most exciting day of Marie's life. She couldn't wait to tell her family all about it; but just as she was about to rush home, something happened that almost spoiled her happiness.

At the back of the big room, someone started shouting. A girl ran past Marie in tears. She was followed by a fierce, gray-bearded man, dressed in expensive clothes.

"Why can't you keep still?" he shouted. "How can I draw you when you keep moving?"

Marie was frightened.

"Who is that bad-tempered man?" she whispered to the girl beside her.

"You will soon find out if you are a pupil here. That is Degas, painter of horses and dancers, and he treats them all the same."

*At the museum, a large crowd has gathered around
the statue of the little ballerina.*

*"Look at her," says the guard. "Look at little Marie.
I'll tell you something—if you stare at her long enough,
she almost seems to move!"*

*"So, did she get her place at the ballet school?"
someone asks.*

"Oh, yes," says the guard, "she got her place all right. She worked hard, practicing her pirouettes and whatnot. In fact, she became so good that the old teacher began to talk about giving her the star part in the Christmas Ballet at the Opera House..."

. . . Marie's dream was coming true.

And even old Degas didn't seem quite so frightening. Every day he turned up with his top hat and his sketch books, muttering and cursing everyone. He worked furiously with colored chalks, sketching the girls, the teachers, and the musicians.

"Keep still!" he would shout. "Not like that. Like this . . . !" Then he would show some poor dancer how to hold a pose or to skip properly.

Marie had to try hard not to laugh at the sight of the smartly dressed painter balancing on one leg.

Sometimes, Marie caught a glimpse of his sketches,
and what she saw made her gasp—the drawings almost
glowed with color. There were studies of all the girls,
but they didn't look like ballet stars.

Degas had drawn them...

chattering,

stretching,

tying their laces,

adjusting their straps—

even reading
a newspaper.

Marie loved her dancing. She was the first to arrive
in the morning and the last to go home at night.

Then, one day, everything started to go wrong.

Marie's father became ill, and soon he couldn't work
anymore. Her mother took in extra washing, but there
simply wasn't enough money to pay for all Marie's classes.

Her dream of becoming a famous dancer began to fade.

"I would love to help you, Marie," said the kind
old teacher, "but unless you have lessons every day
I will have to give the main part to someone else.
Perhaps we could find a little work for you, sweeping
the floor in the theater or..."

A gruff voice interrupted them.

"I will give you a few francs if you pose for me,
but you will have to work very hard and not chatter.
Do you understand?"

So Degas began to draw Marie every afternoon. He made her stand absolutely still for such a long time that Marie almost cried, but she didn't dare to complain.

The money was not enough. It paid for a doctor for her father, but not for the classes Marie needed. As the Christmas Ballet drew near, she knew she would never have the chance to become famous.

When the big night came, poor Marie was not even allowed to watch, because Degas wanted to work late.

While the other girls laughed and chattered and made themselves ready, Marie was left alone with the artist. More irritable than ever, he made her stand, looking up at the ceiling, with her hands behind her back. All the dancers were used to this pose, but as Degas worked on and on, Marie's neck began to ache.

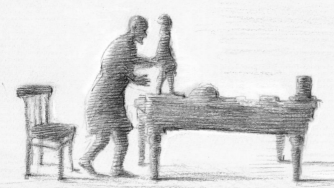

It was getting late.

"Excuse me, Monsieur Degas," Marie whispered. "I will have to go home soon. My father is ill and my family will be worried."

"Family!" shouted Degas. "Your family will be worried? Do you know who will worry about me? No one, that's who. I have only my work for company and now even my eyesight is leaving me."

"I'm sorry, Monsieur, I don't understand."

Degas worked in silence for a while. He pulled out some clay and began to work furiously with his long fingers. Then Marie saw a tear in the artist's eye.

"No," he said more gently, "how could you understand? Tell me, Marie, what is the most precious thing to a painter?"

"Your eyes, Monsieur?"

"Exactly. My eyes! Just like a dancer's legs,
you understand? And *my* poor eyes are sick, Marie.
That is why I am working with clay, because I can
hardly see what I am doing anymore."

Suddenly Marie felt very sad for the bad-tempered
artist. Could this be why he was always angry?

"I am very sorry," she said.

Then Degas did something Marie had never seen
him do before. He looked up at her and smiled.

"I am sorry, too, Marie," he said. "But look at
the sculpture. It's the best thing I've ever done. Thank you,
my little dancer. Now you must go home."

Marie stepped down. Her legs were weak.
She untied the peach-colored ribbon
from her hair and gave it to the old artist.
Then she put away her dancing clothes
and ran home to her family.

In the theater, the crowds clapped and cheered
as the curtain came down on the Christmas Ballet.
Outside, under a pale streetlight, an old, nearly blind
artist struggled home alone.

In his hand he clutched a peach-colored ribbon.

"*And so she never did find her dream?*" someone asks.
"*Wait,*" says the guard. "*The story isn't quite finished…*"

Two years later Marie was helping her mother with
the laundry when a letter arrived at 36, Rue de Douai.

"It's for you, Marie," said her mother.

Marie tore open the envelope. Inside was a ticket
and an invitation to a big art exhibition. On the invitation
someone had scribbled "For Marie, the little dancer."

Marie and her mother went to the show. The building was very crowded. The walls were hung with brilliantly colored paintings, but the biggest crowd was gathered around a large glass box.

Marie pushed through the crowd.

"Look!" she gasped. " It's me!"

Degas had dressed the sculpture in real clothes. No one had seen anything like it before. In her hair was the peach-colored ribbon.

At the museum the last person has gone home and
the guard wipes a little dust from the dancer's shoe.
    "Good night, Marie," he says, and he walks away,
whistling to himself.
        As the keys turn in the lock, the little dancer
            almost seems to smile. The rain on the museum
                roof sounds like a thousand hands clapping—
                    clapping for Marie, the most famous
                        dancer in the world.

EDGAR DEGAS (1834-1917) was born in Paris, the eldest son of a wealthy banker.
As a young man, he studied drawing in Paris and Italy, and soon became
well known for his pictures of racehorses, his nudes and, of course, his ballet
dancers, which made up half his work. He was also very keen on printmaking
and photography.

He sold many pictures and was a great collector of other artists' work, owning
such famous paintings as Van Gogh's *Sunflowers*. Although he never married, he
thought of the paintings in his collection as his "children."

Degas was a bad-tempered man who upset many people, although he would often
apologize afterward. He spent hours observing and sketching, totally absorbed
in his work.

As his eyesight worsened, he turned from oil painting to large pastel drawings,
and began modeling with wax and clay. In 1880 he asked Marie van Goethen,
a young pupil at the Opera Ballet School in Paris, to pose for him. The finished wax
model of *The Little Dancer*, fully clothed and wearing a real wig, was the only Degas
sculpture to be exhibited during his lifetime. It was displayed in a glass case at the
Impressionist Exhibition of 1881, where its extraordinary realism created a sensation.

The original sculpture of *The Little Dancer* is now in the Louvre in Paris. After
Degas' death, the model was cast in bronze, and more than twenty copies were made.
Some of those bronzes can be seen in the collections of major museums and galleries
around the world.

Edgar Degas

Marie dreams of becoming the most famous ballerina
in the world, but it is hard to find enough money
for lessons. At last she begins modeling for the artist
Edgar Degas, well-known for his paintings of dancers
and horses and for his fiery temper. When his beautiful
sculpture of "The Little Dancer" is finished, Marie's
dream comes true.

Complete with reproductions of Degas' work, this
is another inspirational story from Laurence Anholt's
bestselling series, celebrating some of the world's
greatest artists and the real children who knew them.

ANHOLT'S ARTISTS

BARRON'S

ISBN-13: 978-0-7641-3852-2
ISBN-10: 0-7641-3852-9

EAN

9 780764 138522

50899>

$8.99   Canada $10.99
www.barronseduc.com

The Magical Garden of

Claude Monet

LAURENCE ANHOLT